WIZARD'S
WEEKEND COTTAGE

THE
HAUNTED
CABIN

DEPARTMENT
OF DEPORTMENT

PERFECT
PICNIC
SPOT

LITTLE LAKE

THE ONLY ROAD

FISHING
SPOT

THIS WAY
TO
OTHERVILLE

THE BEWILDERNESS

This book is for Mose, who asked for a book with
dragons, robots, superheroes, AND kittens.
—L.S.

To Julien and Frankie
—A.D.

An Imprint of Rodale Books
400 South Tenth Street, Emmaus, PA 18098
Visit us online at www.rodalekids.com

Text © 2017 by Laurel Snyder
Illustrations © 2017 by Aurore Damant

Rodale books may be purchased for business or promotional use or for special sales.
For information, write to: Trade Books/Special Markets Dept., Rodale Inc., 733 Third Avenue, NY, NY 10017

Printed in China; Manufactured by RRD Asia 201702

Design by Yeon Kim
Text set in Mrs. Ant
The artwork for this book was created digitally using Photoshop

Library of Congress Cataloging-in-Publication Data is on file with the publisher.
ISBN-13: 978-1-62336-874-6
Distributed to the trade by Macmillan
10 9 8 7 6 5 4 3 2 1 hardcover

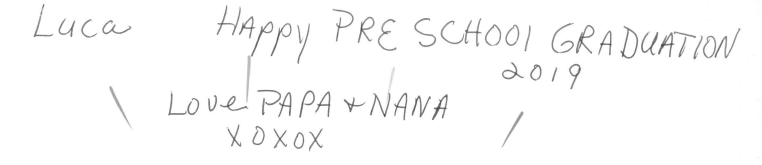

The King of TOO MANY THINGS

Words by
Laurel Snyder

Pictures by
Aurore Damant

RODALE KiDS

Once upon a time in a small kingdom, with an even smaller king...

Jasper had a good thing going.
It was fun being the king.

Every morning, he ruled from his throne of pillows.
And each afternoon, he spent a few hours reading, coloring,
and having a snack with Greg!

It was nice.

But one morning, Jasper woke up…
wanting *more*.

His books seemed boring.

His crayons were dull—even his
favorite gold crayon.

"You know what we need?" he said to the Wizard. "A dragon!"

"A dragon?" asked the Wizard.

"Sure!" said Jasper. "Dragons are **exciting**.

Everything's better with dragons!"

"I'm not so certain," said the Wizard.

But Jasper was the king.

And so... *poof!*

ONE EXCITING DRAGON!

The dragon dazzled. He did loop-da-loops in the throne room.
He shot through the window and into the sky.

But as Jasper watched, a rosebush down in the courtyard burst into flames!

Suddenly, there were tiny fires **everywhere.**

"Yikes!" Jasper shouted, dashing outside.
"This is not what I meant by **exciting!**
Do something! Turn him off!"

"Sorry," said the Wizard.
"I don't know how to turn off a dragon."
Jasper stared at the flames.

Then he snapped his fingers. "I know—**robots!**"

"Robots?" asked the Wizard.

"Robots will stomp out the fires!"
said Jasper.

"Robots will save the day. Robots will be
terrific!"

"I'm not so certain," said the Wizard.

But Jasper was the king.

And so... *poof!*

TWO TERRIFIC ROBOTS!

The robots did put out the fires.

They also trudged and trampled
everything in sight.
Small children ran away in fear.

"These robots are a problem!" cried Jasper. "Try something else!"
"Like what?" asked the Wizard.

"Superheroes!" said Jasper.
"Superheroes?" asked the Wizard.
Jasper nodded.

"Superheroes can fix *anything*.
They're **super**."

"I'm not so certain," said the Wizard.
But Jasper was the king.
And so... *poof!*

THREE SUPER SUPERHEROES!

"Catch that dragon!" said Jasper.

"Stop those robots!"

The superheroes tied up the robots.

They put the dragon on a handy leash.

They even took Jasper for a ride.

But when the kids of the kingdom saw Jasper flying,
they wanted a ride, too. Soon, boys and girls were shouting
all over town. They wailed from trees and porches.
They refused to eat their dinners.

"Me! Pick me!"

The **Wizard** developed a headache.

"This is not **super** anymore," said Jasper.

"Now what?"

"Don't look at me," replied the Wizard.

"You're the king."

"I know! **Kittens!**"

"Kittens?" asked the Wizard.

"Everyone loves kittens," said Jasper. "Kittens will stop the wailing. We need kittens!"

"Couldn't we just put everyone in time-out?" asked the Wizard. Jasper shook his head.

"Kittens!" he insisted. "Kittens are...

cute!"

The Wizard could hardly argue with *that*.
Anyway, Jasper was the king.
And so... *poof!*

CUTE KITTENS EVERYWHERE!

"Meow?"

One by one, the kids stopped wailing.
Because it's true—*everyone* loves kittens.

But Jasper still had a problem.
Or four...
The kittens teased the dragon, who spit sparks.

The kittens pounced the robots, who clanked furiously.

The kittens climbed the Superheroes, shredding their tights.

And... the kittens licked the **butter!**

Then there was Greg. "Oh, poor Greg!" cried Jasper. "This won't do. Wizard!"

But the Wizard was nowhere to be seen.
"Wizard?"

So Jasper grabbed Greg and ran away from the kittens and the mess and the noise and the fire and the clanking.

He ran all the way back to the castle and his quiet throne of pillows.

A few minutes later, there was a knock at the door.
"Who is it?" asked Jasper.

"I'm Janey," said Janey. "From down the street. I'm just returning your kitten. He makes me sneezy."

"Oh, wow. I made a big mess, huh?" asked Jasper.

"You sure did," said Janey. "A real **cat-astrophe.**"

"I'm sorry," said Jasper. "How can I make it up to you?"
"Well, I *could* use a snack," said Janey.

When Jasper returned, Janey was busy.
And Greg was sound asleep.

After a while, Jasper looked up from his drawing.
"Hey," he said. "This is nice."

"It *is* nice," said Janey. "But do you know what might be even nicer?"

Jasper shook his head emphatically. "**Nothing!**" he said.
"Absolutely nothing! Nothing at all. Nice is nice enough!"

"But . . . you're the king!" said Janey. "You could wish
for *anything*. Don't you want anything more?"

Jasper considered her question. "Well," he admitted at last. "I guess there is *one* thing.

I *could* use some help cleaning up all that mess..."

And so it was that Jasper made a friend, Janey got a snack, and Greg took a much-needed nap. After that, they rolled up their sleeves and did a little picking up.

Well, more than a little.

But *then* they lived happily ever after.

Only now with a few more kittens.

THE END.